Disney's
WINNIE THE POOH
CHRISTMAS

TREASURY

Disney
PRESS

NEW YORK

✴ Contents ✴

"**I** LOVE THE NIGHT BEFORE CHRISTMAS!" exclaimed Christopher Robin as he and Pooh, bundled warmly in bright-colored mufflers and black, shiny boots, walked side by side through the snow-covered Hundred-Acre Wood. "Don't you, Pooh Bear?"

"Why, yes," responded Pooh thoughtfully, "now that you mention it, I do." Then, like a balloon blocking the sun, the bear's brow furrowed into a frown. "But . . ." he murmured.

"But *what*, Pooh?" Christopher Robin wanted to know.

"Isn't *every* night a night before one Christmas or another?" Pooh asked, rubbing his suddenly muddled head. "Sort of?"

"Well," answered a surprised Christopher Robin, "that is true, Pooh Bear. Sort of."

Christopher Robin stopped walking and looked down at Pooh, who also stopped walking.

"But I'm talking about Christmas *Eve*," explained Christopher Robin carefully, "and about all the things that happen on that night that make it so very special."

"Ah!" exclaimed Pooh, finally understanding. And as they continued their walk, the bear of little brain but bountiful appetite considered the things he loved about this night. And a certain Christmas Eve popped out of his memory that was very special because he had had the opportunity to do more of the things that made *every* night, for Pooh Bear, a little bit of the night before Christmas.

His tummy remembered, too, and rumbled its recollection of . . .

The Bite Before Christmas

'Twas the night before Christmas
With snow soft and new,
Not a creature was stirring
Except Winnie the Pooh!

The bear of little brain was dressed warmly in his favorite flannel nightshirt with its matching cap (topped by a very snazzy red tassel) and was tucked cozily into bed with quilts, blankets, and sheets pulled snugly up under his chin.

But his eyes were wide open and staring (because that's what wide-open eyes do), and sleep was the last thing on his mind.

"Oh bother," he said, sighing. And, as if to emphasize his restlessness, he immediately followed it with "Oh BOTHER, bother!"

Surprisingly, it wasn't the imminent arrival of Christmas, the tingling anticipation of tomorrow morning's full stocking dangling from the mantel, or the beribboned presents piled under the tree, that were keeping the bear awake.

No, what was bouncing about in the fluff of Pooh's head was the same thing that was bouncing about in it at this particular time *every* night.

"A small smackerel of something sweet," Pooh said dreamily, smacking his lips.

Pooh worked very hard at making sure his honey and his day ran out at the same time. But in the middle of the night, *every* night, like some sort of internal alarm clock, Pooh Bear's tummy would begin to rumble and growl until the entire bed appeared to be buzzing and vibrating. He tried his best not to notice, knowing that daytime was for eating and nighttime was for sleeping.

But this was what Pooh called the hungry part of the night, and there was simply no ignoring it if you were a bear to whom the world was a place where it was *always* time for breakfast!

"And a very nice sort of world it is, too," Pooh said as he sat up in bed.

Tossing back his covers, Pooh slid out from beneath the bedclothes and dropped feetfirst into the slippers waiting patiently by the bed. *Thumpety-thump, thumpety-thump,* the slippers echoed on the hard wooden floors as the bear headed for his favorite part of his house—his favorite part of any house, for that matter—the kitchen!

There was no need to light a candle or a lamp because a full moon gleamed across the new snow blanketing the wood outside, making night appear as bright as day!

Pooh's face fell, however, at the sight that greeted him upon his arrival in the kitchen. It was a most unhappy collection of dirty dishes, soiled silverware, and spotted saucepans. He'd forgotten to remember the mess he'd made preparing, tasting, baking, tasting, tasting again, and packing all the Christmas treats he'd cooked for his friends, treats that they would allow him to help eat after all the presents were unwrapped tomorrow. In the meantime, however, his kitchen was turned inside out, and his pantry was

decidedly and undeniably as empty as his stomach.

"Oh my goodness gracious," said Pooh, sighing as his tummy emitted such a growl that it set the dishes, piled haphazardly into precarious towers, rattling in sympathy. "If this is a dream, I'd like to wake up right now, if that's quite all right with whoever is in charge of dreaming, of course."

He closed his eyes for a moment to let the dream disappear. But when he squinted one eye open for a peek and saw that nothing had changed from its former untidiness, he knew a bad dream wasn't the problem.

Pooh's head was quite willing to accept this great disappointment and return quietly to bed, but his middle was not being nearly so reasonable. It growled and hummed and gurgled, kicking up such a fuss that Pooh could almost see his tummy churning underneath his nightshirt.

"No doubt about it," murmured Pooh, "someone's going to have to do something about this. And since Pooh Bear, which is me, is the only someone about, I suppose I . . . I mean, him . . . er, me . . . WE are going to be the one . . . two . . . to do it!" He scrunched his forehead into a frown and scratched his ear fiercely. He was very glad there was only one of him because counting any higher was not something he did very well. "But what are we . . . am I . . . to do?"

All at once, an idea occurred so quickly that Pooh almost didn't realize what it was! Ideas not being something he was very used to having occur at *any* time, it was especially disconcerting to have one happen along when he truly needed it! It was so sudden, in fact, and so unexpected, that Pooh almost forgot it even while it was taking place. The only thing that saved it from drifting away to where most of Pooh's ideas disappeared was the simple fact that it involved food. Food was something Pooh's tummy was simply not going to allow him to forget, no matter how stuffed with fluff a bear's *head* happened to be.

What Pooh remembered was a certain snack.

When Christmas Eve arrived, *everyone* was anxious that Santa not go hungry during his long night's work. Rabbit always set out a steaming bowl of his flavorful vegetable stew. Piglet, who could never make up his mind as to what Santa might find the most appetizing, provided a mug of hot cocoa and a list of what was to be found in his very small but well-stocked pantry, along with an invitation for Santa to help himself!

Pooh thought a snack was a good idea at any time, even when it wasn't for him. So every

Christmas Eve, he placed a plateful of homemade gingerbread snowmen and a big glass of frosty milk on the hearth in expectation of Santa's need for a rest after packing the sackful of mostly edible presents Pooh was always in hopes of receiving all the way from the North Pole!

Thumpety-thump, thumpety-thump, thumpety-THUMP! Pooh scurried toward the living room, licking his lips in anticipation. He was certain that Santa wouldn't begrudge him one little cookie—perhaps two—and a small sip of cold milk.

In less time than it takes to eat a plate of cookies and empty a glass of milk (which is hardly any time at all in Pooh's house), Pooh was sprawled in his favorite armchair, his feet perched comfortably upon the ottoman, an empty glass of milk in one

hand, half of the last gingerbread snowman cookie in the other, and a frothy milk mustache under his nose!

Needless to say, Pooh was at this moment quite cozy, and his tummy was, temporarily at least, quite satisfied. He leaned his head against the back of the chair and let his mind consider one of the truly important questions in the life of a bear of little brain.

"Why is it," Pooh asked himself while stifling a very insistent yawn, "that we have TWO hands for stuffing honey, but only ONE mouth to stuff?"

The only answer that came to him was the prodigious yawn that simply refused stifling.

The next thing the bear knew, he was being shaken gently awake by a cold hand. He lifted his sleepy eyelids, and his eyes immediately opened with an amazed *pop* at what they saw! It was Santa Claus, leaning over Pooh and smiling happily into his face!

"Oh!" said Pooh with a gasp, because "oh!" is what is usually said when a surprise takes place.

"Pooh Bear!" exclaimed Santa, ceasing to shake him. "I certainly am glad to see you! Ho-ho-ho!"

"You are?" responded the bear, more than a bit disconcerted because that's exactly what he was going to say to Santa—except for the ho-ho-ho part, of course.

"Oh my goodness, yes," said Santa, sighing in what seemed to be great relief. "In fact, I had just decided my problem was quite

important enough to wake you." Santa placed his hand on Pooh's shoulder. "I need your help," he announced solemnly.

Pooh's ears instantly pricked up to listen to what the jolly old elf had to say. But, Pooh thought to himself, how can I possibly help Santa Claus?

"It's all these wonderful snacks," answered Santa as if Pooh had asked the question aloud. "Everyone has thoughtfully left me goodies, goodies, and more goodies to refresh me on my rounds. Well, I still have a very long way to go, and . . ." he said, sighing heavily, ". . . I'm FULL!"

Pooh blinked his eyes rapidly in surprise. Being FULL was a feeling with which he was not at all familiar. This was quite all right with him, however, because he'd always found the "doing" of a thing much more exciting than the "having done" part, especially when what one was doing was eating, whether breakfast or lunch or dinner or any small (or large) sort of smackerel in between!

"And," Santa continued, "it's very important not to hurt anyone's feelings." He looked Pooh Bear in the eye. "Do you suppose you and your appetite could come along with me tonight and help me with some of this food?"

A happy smile spread itself over Pooh's face, and his tummy agreed with a particularly enthusiastic rumble.

Santa smiled back, his eyes twinkling merrily.

"Ho-ho-HO!" Santa laughed. "That sounds like a YES to me!"

The next thing Pooh knew, he was seated next to Santa in the toy-laden sleigh, wearing his slippers, nightshirt, and cap (still topped with its snazzy red tassel), and snuggled comfortably beneath a fuzzy blanket.

"Ready?" inquired Santa with a grin.

"I suppose I am," said Pooh, nodding nervously.

A slight flick of Santa's wrists sent the reindeer soaring into the air in an explosion of chiming sleigh bells.

Within a very short time, Pooh was eating yam cake and drinking root beer in front of the sleeping Gopher's fire as Santa

filled the stocking dangling from the mantel.

At Tigger's, while the sounds of feline snoring resounded from the bedroom, Santa went about his business, and Pooh dined on oatmeal cookies striped with rows of chocolate chips.

The snack at Kanga and Roo's house consisted of a great many very small peanut butter cookies and a dainty cup of lemon tea.

By the time they left Eeyore's house and the remnants of his bowlful of brownies, flying off into the world beyond the Hundred-Acre Wood, Pooh Bear was losing track of what was being eaten where!

The night became a blur of whirling flights and good things to eat. One moment Santa was whizzing past the moon, the next Pooh was seated comfortably in one strange living room or another, slurping noodles in China, sipping hot onion soup with melted cheese in France, devouring Danish pastries in Denmark, and licking luscious ice cream in Iceland!

Soon, even the bottomless Pooh was unable to distinguish one country from another because all he knew was that he was truly full at last and couldn't possibly eat another bite. This might have made anyone else sad, but Pooh knew, as certainly as bees meant honey and Christmas meant Santa Claus, that tomorrow morning the arrival of breakfast would coincide with his being ready to eat it. He was, however, a bit uneasy about whether or not there would be anything at home to serve at the anticipated breakfast.

"Don't worry, Pooh," said Santa as he clapped the bear on the back, "we won't let any of this food go to waste!"

Thereafter, as a bag was emptied of toys, it was refilled with all sorts of savories, sweets, stews, soups, and sauces!

As this went on and on, Pooh sat beneath his fuzzy blanket with a big smile on his face and a warm feeling in his middle. The swoops and twirls of the flying sleigh, the wind rushing against his closed eyes, the ho-ho-ho-ing from Santa as he shouted encouragement to his reindeer blended together and drifted away until it all seemed like such a . . . DREAM?

Pooh sat up, suddenly wide awake, only to discover that he was in his own bed with a sparkling Christmas morning shining through the windows into his bedroom. He didn't remember going to bed, but, as Tigger would tease him, not 'memberin' is one o' the things Pooh Bears do best!

"It was all a dream," he said. "And a very nice one, at that!"

Then he smiled and patted his middle. "Such a good dream that even my tummy was fooled into thinking it's not hungry."

His tummy responded with a low rumble.

"Well," Pooh said with a chuckle, "not VERY hungry."

Immediately, Winnie the Pooh jumped out of bed and, ignoring his slippers, went slipping and sliding across the polished wooden floors into his kitchen. There he found not a single dish or pot or saucepan dirty or out of place! And his pantry! Oh, his pantry! It was crammed from top to bottom with food from all over the world.

"Oh my!" said Pooh wonderingly. "Where did all this come from?" Then the tickle of recollection at the back of his mind burst forth into a giggle as he remembered his wish list to Santa. It had included requests for as many mouthwatering delicacies as he could think of, and there they all were, filling his pantry and, of course, making his mouth water!

"It's better than a dream," Pooh said with a sigh. "Unless, of course, it *is* a dream," he added, with a puzzled frown.

"But whether it's a dream, or merely a wonderful Christmas, which is pretty much the same thing," Pooh murmured happily to himself, "I hope neither one ends before I've eaten!"

Then the realization descended on the suddenly overawed little bear of what was an even more wonderful present than a pantry full of everything he'd asked for. What better way to celebrate Christmas than with a memory, even the memory of a dream, of helping someone like Santa Claus, who spent all his time helping others?

"What a special present," exclaimed Pooh, as his tummy filled with a warm feeling and his heart beat just a bit faster. "Because a happy memory, or a good dream, NEVER wears out . . . or needs to be filled up again!"

Pooh could hardly wait to tell his friends. As soon as he got dressed, he decided, he was going to go visit every one of his neighbors in the Hundred-Acre Wood and regale them with his adventure!

Then, the overflowing pantry caught Pooh Bear's eye.

"Well," he said to himself with a chuckle, "right after breakfast!"

Pooh's Christmas Hum

Outside the wind is blowing.

Inside the fire is glowing.

And everyone is going off to sleep

For Christmas Day is coming.

Pum-pum, the drummers are drumming.

Hurrah! I'll go on humming, since I'm Pooh.

Santa Pooh

This Christmas Eve while sitting
In my oh-so-thoughtful spot,
I had a thought while eating
From my tasty honeypot.

Perhaps I should play Santa Claus
For all my friends this year,
Dropping presents at their doorstep
And bringing Christmas cheer.

Tigger wants a bright red ball
That bounces up and down.
Eeyore needs a new pink bow
To wipe away his frown.

Rabbit wants new gardening tools
To help him sow and till.
Piglet needs more haycorns,
So that he can have his fill.

And everyone will *ooh* and *aah*
When they come to visit me,
'Cause there'll be so many presents
Underneath my Christmas tree!

The Night Before Christmas

'Twas the night before Christmas,
when all through the house
Not a creature was stirring,
not even a mouse;
The stockings were hung
by the chimney with care,
In hopes that St. Nicholas
soon would be there;

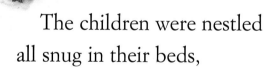

The children were nestled
all snug in their beds,
While visions of sugarplums
danced in their heads;
And Piglet in his kerchief,
and I in my cap,
Had just settled our brains
for a long winter's nap,

When out on the lawn
there arose such a clatter,
    I sprang from my bed
to see what was the matter.
    Away to the window I flew
like a flash,
    Tore open the shutters
and threw up the sash.

When what to my wondering
eyes should appear,
    But a miniature sleigh and
eight tiny reindeer,
    With a little old driver, so
lively and quick,
    I knew in a moment it must
be St. Nick.

More rapid than eagles
his coursers they came,
    And he whistled
and shouted, and called
them by name:
    "Now, Dasher! Now,
Dancer! Now, Prancer and Vixen!
    On, Comet! On, Cupid! On, Donder
and Blitzen!
    To the top of the porch, to the top of the wall!
    Now dash away, dash away, dash away, all!"

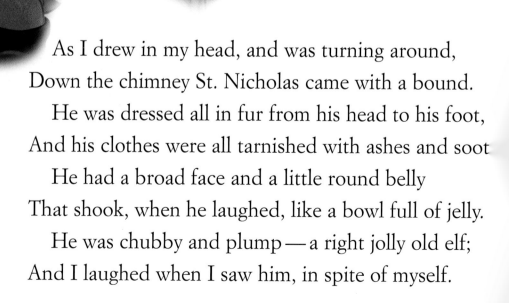

    As I drew in my head, and was turning around,
Down the chimney St. Nicholas came with a bound.
    He was dressed all in fur from his head to his foot,
And his clothes were all tarnished with ashes and soot
    He had a broad face and a little round belly
That shook, when he laughed, like a bowl full of jelly.
    He was chubby and plump — a right jolly old elf;
And I laughed when I saw him, in spite of myself.

He spoke not a word,
but went straight to his work,
   And filled all the stockings;
then turned with a jerk,
   And laying his finger aside
of his nose,
   And giving a nod, up the
chimney he rose.

He sprang to his sleigh,
to his team gave a whistle,
   And away they all flew
like the down of a thistle;
   But I heard him exclaim,
ere he drove out of sight,
   "Happy Christmas to all,
and to all a good night!"

A Tigger at Christmastime

The most fabulous thing for a tigger
Is wrapping up fabulous things.

First I wrap 'em in paper,
Then I tie 'em with strings.

Cutting, taping, folding, tying—
Ho-ho-ho-ho-ho!

But the most fabulous things for a tigger
Are the smiles of friends I know.

A Very Small Christmas

Piglet loved *almost* everything about the night before Christmas. There was, for instance, the beautifully decorated Christmas tree that needn't be very tall or very wide. It could actually be a very small tree that suited the very small Piglet very well indeed (even if the tippity-top was still out of reach).

And there were all the unopened presents spread out beneath the tree and hidden about the house: stashed under the bed, tucked away in the back of a drawer, and nestled safely out of reach atop the shelves of the linen closet. Piglet so appreciated the looks of an artistically papered and beribboned present that he often wrapped and bowed empty boxes simply because of the Christmassy feeling they gave his home. And, later, amid all the unwrapping (during which he was ever so careful not to tear the paper so it could be used again next year), he was occasionally surprised by a gift to which he'd treated himself and then forgotten all about! Piglet's very small memory was another thing he loved about Christmas.

But the aspect of Christmas Eve that Piglet cherished most was the candles! Candles alight everywhere, flickering as decorations

on the tree and lined up smartly across the mantel (right above his freshly starched and pressed—and very small—Christmas stocking), arranged according to size with a tall, thin candle on one end and a short, squat one on the other, all glowing cozily.

On a table next to his upholstered armchair (which had a ruffle around the bottom) sat another candle, as thick as a barber pole and sporting the same red, white, and blue stripes and topped by a bright yellow flame.

There were candles in the kitchen, candles in the corridor, candles in the bedroom, and candles in the bath. With so many candles burning all at once, Piglet was especially careful to make certain that no accidents happened to his candles, to himself, or to his very small but brightly illuminated home.

The warm, waxy glimmerings so pleased Piglet that he always waited until the last moment to kindle a fire in the fireplace so as not to spoil too soon the flickering candle lights playing across the walls and ceilings. It made him feel safe and serene and cared for, which helped him not to think about the one thing Piglet did *not* like about the night before Christmas. It was the same thing he didn't like about *any* night. They were all so very, VERY dark!

"You never realize," said Piglet, sighing to himself in a tiny voice, "how short a day is until you're afraid of the dark."

Piglet's consolation was that this Christmas he'd asked Santa to bring him a night-light to keep him company on all the dark nights to come. In the meantime, his candles would provide him with companionship until, just before he fell asleep, he would carefully extinguish every one (candles needed their rest, too) and toss and turn restlessly on the edge of sleep for the remainder of the dark, candleless night while Santa delivered his gifts.

A yawn suddenly widened Piglet's very small mouth into a round, sleepy O, and he stretched contentedly in the warm glow of his candles. Yawns never bothered Piglet. And, although he

always covered his mouth politely when they made themselves known, he was glad when they came.

"A yawn," he said, chuckling to himself, "is simply a smile caught with its mouth open."

Suddenly, a small scratching sounded outside his snugly locked and bolted front door!

Piglet dove for cover! When he found himself safely out of sight beneath his favorite upholstered armchair (with the ruffle around the bottom), he told himself in as reassuring a voice as such a very small animal could manage, "Perhaps it was simply the wind," which was a very real possibility because it was quite a blustery Christmas Eve.

He wasn't reassured for long, however. The scratching sounded again in a most insistent—and very unwindlike—manner!

Piglet breathed a deep, gulping sigh of woe.

"I suppose," he murmured, "that I should go see who"—he paused to gulp nervously—"or WHAT it is!" A small start and squeak of surprise escaped him when the scratching came again, as if agreeing that this was a very good idea, indeed!

As Piglet crawled out from under the upholstered armchair (with the ruffle around the bottom), an idea occurred to him.

"I don't have to open the door to see," he told himself with relief. "I can simply take a very small peek out the window."

Pushing a stool up to the windowsill just off to one side of his front door, Piglet clambered atop it and cautiously peered out through the glass. The door, however, was too much to one side for him to see clearly, no matter how he flattened his nose against the icy cold windowpanes.

"I suppose," he said, breathing softly to himself, "it wouldn't hurt to open the window just a very small smidgen of an opening."

But as soon as Piglet slid open the window just the tiniest bit, a huge gust of wind chose that moment to blast through the crack and see what Christmas Eve was like on the *inside* of a house!

Now, as is well known, gently flickering candle flames and rough gusts of rambunctious breeze are not the most amiable of acquaintances.

In no time at all, the mischievous breeze blew through the living room, wafted around the kitchen, bustled into the bedroom, blasted out of the bath, and exited out the window that Piglet had been too surprised to close until the damage had been done.

Every candle in Piglet's house had been extinguished and, if it were possible, it was now darker inside than out in the night of moaning wind.

"At least," the frightened Piglet stammered to himself, "I certainly *hope* it's the wind that's moaning."

Suddenly, the scratching sounded once again and, to Piglet's great surprise, he noticed a small, fluttering light—not inside his house but emerging dimly, then brightly, then dimly again through the crack beneath his securely fastened front door!

Oh my! thought Piglet. If there is light on the outside, then I'd be very foolish not to open the door and let it in!

Without hesitating another moment, the very small—but oh-so-very-brave—Piglet unlocked, unbolted, and threw open the heavy portal, letting in the billowing breeze!

Piglet watched in amazement as a small flickering light blew into his house, caught in the breeze's grip and swirling and spinning out of control about the living room ceiling! Desperately trying to escape the clutches of the rowdy breeze, the flickering spot of light managed to grab hold and cling to the tip-top of Piglet's Christmas tree, where it swayed back and forth, glimmering determinedly while the wind tried in vain to loosen its grip.

Piglet, frozen in awe at the still open door, watched the struggle in openmouthed wonder. That very high (even on his very small tree), very pointy part had always been a great disappointment to him because he could never reach high enough to decorate it properly. And now this mysterious light had arrived under such strange circumstances and made his tree more like Christmas than he'd ever thought possible!

It took a moment for Piglet to recover from his amazement at the light's presence and slam the front door shut. As soon as the door began to close, of course, the pesky wind darted back outside where it felt most at home, leaving Piglet alone with the light twittering vigorously atop the Christmas tree, as though trying to regain its breath after the long struggle with the vexing breeze.

Piglet, now that his home was illuminated by the eerie yet warmly appealing light, was hesitant to relight his candles and spoil the marvelous show, almost like a display of tiny fireworks.

He held out toward the light a plate of cookies cut into Christmas shapes.

"Would you care for some refreshments?" Piglet asked politely. "You're very welcome here. In fact," Piglet continued, trying not to blush with embarrassment, "I'm very glad you came."

As if in response, the light drifted down and settled gossamerlike at the tip of a Christmas-tree-shaped cookie. Now Piglet could see that it wasn't just a light, but a tiny firefly. He couldn't tell if the insect was actually eating the cookie, but its

light seemed to grow stronger, as if simply being close to a friendly someone was all the nourishment it needed. Piglet smiled. He knew that feeling well. It was one of his favorites.

"It seems," Piglet suggested, making polite conversation, "that you've been surprised by the arrival of winter."

The lightning bug shimmered his agreement.

"Well," said Piglet, "you're quite welcome to stay as long as you like."

He picked up a candle in its holder, intending to light his way to bed with it as soon as he had found a match.

"It's long past my bedtime," explained Piglet to the glowing firefly, "so, if you'll excuse me, I must be off to sleep."

Before he could leave, however, the firefly fluttered up and perched on the cold wick of the unlit candle in Piglet's hand, blinking a question.

"Why, of course you may come with me," responded Piglet.

And so Piglet had the very best night's sleep, Christmas Eve or otherwise, that he'd ever had, with his houseguest twinkling merrily on his bedpost to the accompaniment of some very small snores.

The next morning, *Christmas* morning, Piglet and the firefly were up with the sun, going through the presents stuffed in Piglet's stocking. As Piglet reached the bottom, however, a look of consternation crossed his face.

"Oh dear," he said with a sigh. "Santa forgot to give me my night-light. And that's what I wanted the most."

The bug sparkled sympathetically.

"He forgot your present, too?" asked Piglet in surprise. "What did you ask him for?"

The bug blinked in response.

"A home out of the winter wind," murmured Piglet.

Suddenly, like the sun rising and chasing off a night full of bad dreams, a thought occurred to Piglet.

"You don't suppose . . ." he began, hardly able to believe such a wonderful idea. "You don't suppose that Santa was making this our best Christmas ever by bringing us together . . . do you?"

The firefly blinked what seemed to Piglet's eyes to be a bright affirmation.

"It simply goes to show," remarked Piglet that night, as the firefly sat glowing contentedly on the bedpost, "that sometimes the very small things at Christmas are the very best things."

And the firefly twinkled his agreement.

Christmas Cookies

Eggs, sugar, flour—
I mix. I stir. I shake.

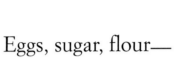

Trees, bells, stars—
I roll. I cut. I bake.

Frosting, sprinkles, candy—
I paint. I pat. I press.

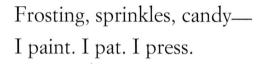

Bowls, pans, crumbs—
I've made a yummy mess!

Eeyore's Christmas Surprise

One especially merry Christmas Eve, Eeyore decorated his house with shiny cranberries, boughs of evergreen, and a festive wreath.

His friends all exclaimed that the little house had never looked better.

But when Eeyore pinned his yellow stocking to the front door, *CREAK*, groaned the door! *RUMBLE*, rattled the roof! *CRASH*, went the house!

"It was too good to last," said Eeyore, sadly pulling his stocking from the pile.

"We can fix the place right up," said Rabbit. "It will just take some organizing."

"And some digging," added Gopher, making holes to hold the beams.

"And some sweeping," chimed in Piglet, cleaning up the new floor.

"And some helping!" shouted all of Eeyore's friends. Everyone rushed to rebuild the house — for how could Santa bring presents, if there was no home to bring them to?

But despite the organizing, digging, sweeping, and helping, Eeyore's house was not finished until after the sun rose on Christmas morning. Had Eeyore missed Christmas?

A glint of yellow caught his eye. It was his stocking, stuffed with gifts for everyone! "I guess Christmas comes wherever there's the Christmas spirit," said Eeyore.

All his friends in the Hundred-Acre Wood cheered. They knew he was right.

A Christmas Tree for Pooh

Christmas Tree,
O Christmas Tree,
Standing in the snow.
Would you like to come with me?
Okay, then, off we'll go.

Christmas Tree,
O Christmas Tree,
With your boughs outspread.
A lovely vision you will be—
Decked out in green and red.

Christmas Tree,
O Christmas Tree,
Wrapped in chains of light.
Now you're dressed for all to see:
Topped with a star so bright!

Pooh's Jingle Bells

"Mmmm, I love Christmas Eve," said Winnie the Pooh, patting his tummy. "Tomorrow, my stocking will be full of brand-new honeypots!"

"Presents are fun," said Christopher Robin, "but getting presents isn't the most important thing about Christmas, you know."

Pooh scratched behind his ear. "I suppose there ARE other things about Christmas," he said, though he couldn't remember any at the moment.

"Christmas is a time for thinking of others and helping," said Christopher Robin.

Pooh thought about Santa delivering presents all over the world. "Nobody needs more help than Santa!" he cried. "If only we had a sleigh, we could help him deliver presents in it!"

"Good thinking," said Christopher Robin. "Let's go see if anyone has a sleigh we can use."

They found Piglet outside his door, sweeping snow and singing:

Jingle bells, jingle bells, jingle all the way!
Oh, what fun it is to ride
in a one-horse open sleigh. . . .

"That's an idea," said Pooh.

"What is?" asked Piglet.

"A one-horse open sleigh," replied Pooh. "That ought to get us to the North Pole."

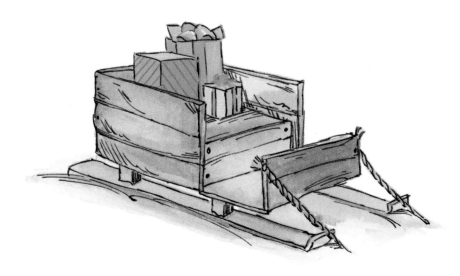

"The N-north Pole!" cried Piglet.

"Yes," said Pooh. "Christopher Robin says Christmas is about helping others, and nobody needs more help than Santa."

"What a grand idea!" cried Piglet. "I'd like to go, too, but I have to finish clearing my walk."

"We can help you with that," said Christopher Robin.

Together they shoveled until the snow was piled up neatly on both sides of Piglet's path.

"Now, let's go and see if Kanga knows anything about a sleigh," said Pooh.

They found Roo in his front yard, jingling his jingle bells.

"Oh!" cried Piglet. "Jingle bells are just what we need for our one-horse open sleigh!"

"A sleigh! A sleigh!" sang Roo. "Where is it?"

"Well, we don't exactly have it yet," explained Pooh. "But when we do, we're going to take it to the North Pole and help Santa deliver presents."

"What a nice idea," said Kanga.

"Do you have a sleigh we can borrow?" asked Christopher Robin.

"No," said Kanga, "but Tigger's coming over soon. I'm sure he'll let you borrow his. Now come in and warm yourselves, while I bake these Christmas cookies."

"Can we help you make them?" asked Pooh.

"Certainly, dear," said Kanga.

Together, they sifted flour and spices—then they stirred in butter and honey. And soon the delicious smell of cookies was coming from Kanga's oven.

"Mmmmmm, yummy!" cried Tigger as he bounced through the front door.

For a while, the cookies made everyone forget all about helping Santa. But Piglet suddenly remembered: "Tigger, we need to borrow your sleigh, so we can help Santa deliver his presents."

"When it comes to helping Santa, tiggers are the best!" cried Tigger.

Everyone piled onto Tigger's sled.

Roo jingled his jingle bells.

Everyone sang:

Jingle bells, jingle bells, jingle all the way!

They swooshed down Kanga's hill toward Rabbit's house.

Dashing through the snow,
In a one-horse open sleigh,
O'er the fields we go,
Laughing all the way. . . .

The wind blew and the snowflakes flew. Everyone laughed and shouted.

"Are we at the North Pole yet?" asked Roo, as the sled scrunched to a stop.

"We've been going DOWN for quite some time," said Pooh thoughtfully. "It seems to me the North Pole must be more UP."

Rabbit, Owl, and Eeyore were gathered in front of Rabbit's house. "The North Pole!" exclaimed Rabbit. "You're not even close."

"Besides," said Eeyore, "it's time to decorate the big pine. Or did you forget?" He held up a long cranberry chain.

"Oh yes!" cried Christopher Robin.

Together they hung candy canes and popcorn balls. Then they stood back and admired their beautiful tree.

"What about Santa?" asked Piglet, nudging Pooh.

"Oh!" cried Pooh. "We've got to get to the North Pole to help Santa before it's too late!"

"And you plan to reach the North Pole in this?" asked Owl, pointing to Tigger's sled.

"Yes," said Pooh.

"Well, then, you'll need some locomotion," said Owl.

"A loco-what?" asked Pooh.

"*A horse*, perhaps," said Owl.

"Oh," said Pooh. "We forgot that part!"

Everyone looked at Eeyore.

"Don't look at me," said Eeyore.

"You'd be a great horse!" cried Christopher Robin.

"It's a simple matter of attaching him to the sleigh correctly," said Rabbit. He tied Eeyore to the sled with ropes.

"Not too tight around the middle," Eeyore said, sighing.

"The perfect one-horse open sleigh!" exclaimed Owl, admiring Rabbit's work.

Roo jingled his jingle bells.
Eeyore puffed and pulled.
Everyone sang:

Bells on bobtail ring,
Making spirits bright,
What fun it is to ride and sing
A sleighing song tonight!

Eeyore had trotted happily quite some distance when Christopher Robin noticed that the sun was sinking low in the sky. "I've been thinking," he said. "If we go all the way to the North Pole, we might not have time to give our presents to one another."

"Oh no!" cried Pooh. "Maybe GETTING presents is not the most important thing about Christmas, but GIVING is important."

"Oh d-dear," said Piglet. "I'm sure Santa wouldn't want us to forget that!"

"Keep singing that nice jingly tune," said Eeyore, "and I'll have us around the Hundred-Acre Wood in no time."

Together they laughed and sang and jingled their way from house to house, delivering presents to all their friends.

"We're helping Santa! We're helping Santa!" sang Roo.

"So we are," said Pooh. "We're Santa's helpers after all!"

The Twelve Days of Christmas

On the twelfth day of Christmas
Christopher Robin sent to me

12

Twelve honeybees buzzing

11

Eleven pine trees swaying

10

Ten snowflakes falling

9

Nine jingle bells jingling

8

Eight wreaths for bouncing

7

Seven stockings for hanging

6

Six cards for mailing

5

FIVE POTS OF HONEY

4

Four carrots from Rabbit

3

Three thistles from Eeyore

2

Two Kanga-roos

1

and a Piglet in a pear tree.

Snow Time like Christmas

"But, Mama," moaned the distressed Roo, "how can it be Christmas Eve when there's no snow?"

"It is strange," said Kanga, sighing. "I've never known the Hundred-Acre Wood not to have snow by Christmas."

Kanga and little Roo were looking forlornly out of their open front door at the barren forest. The leaves had all departed long ago, and the carpets of grass had exchanged their crisp green color for somber browns, like children trading their colorful play clothes for warm pajamas.

"You think the snow will ever come, Mama?" Roo asked anxiously. "It just doesn't seem like Christmas at *all*!"

"I don't know, Roo, dear," answered Kanga with a shrug. "Snow, like all weather, has a mind of its own."

Then Kanga smiled down at the woeful expression on her son's face.

"Don't worry, Roo," she told him with a reassuring pat on the head. "Just because the snow is silly enough to miss Christmas doesn't mean we have to."

"Yeah!" said Roo with a laugh. "And if it's really the night

before Christmas, I have some presents to deliver!"

"Whatever do you mean?" asked Kanga.

"Well, you see," began Roo, hopping nervously from one foot to the other as he tried to explain, "I thought it wasn't going to be Christmas till it snowed and that I had plenty of time, so I haven't delivered any of the presents I've gotten for our friends! See?"

Kanga shook her head in exasperated amusement. "Oh dear," she said, sighing. "It's a good thing you didn't wait any longer. I suppose I'll have to—"

"Can I deliver them now, Mama?" interrupted Roo excitedly.

Kanga glanced outside and her brows knitted together into a mother's worried expression.

"It's going to be dark very soon," she began slowly.

Roo, jumping up and down in his excitement, couldn't wait for her to finish.

"I won't get lost, Mama," he protested. "I just *have* to deliver my presents on time! I don't want anyone to think I forgot them on Christmas."

"All right, Roo," answered Kanga with a smile. Then she held up a warning finger. "But promise to stay on the path and come straight home when you're finished."

"Okay, Mama," piped Roo happily in response. "I promise."

Just a very few minutes later, Roo was hopping rapidly down

the path with a sackful of presents for his friends slung over his shoulder.

Then, something cold and wet fell onto the tip of Roo's small nose. Before his startled gaze drifted *another* snowflake with—as is the case of most snowflakes—a great many more drifting right behind it!

"Hurray!" squeaked the delighted Roo. "You made it in time for Christmas, and I'm very glad to see you." He grinned and lifted his face to the falling snow. "And I'm sure everyone else will be, too," he said and poked out his tongue to catch the falling frozen drops of wetness.

And at that very moment, the other inhabitants of the Hundred-Acre Wood were indeed delighting in the descending snow, which grew more and more frenzied, as if all the snowflakes wanted to be on hand for the arrival of Christmas morning.

Winnie the Pooh stuck his head out a window and chuckled as the thickly falling snowflakes seemed to vie with one another for the excitement of plunging down the neck of the bear's red jersey and tickling him into laughter.

From an upper-story window of Rabbit's house, Ol' Long Ears greeted the faster and faster falling snow with a sniff of satisfaction. It was about time the garden got its annual blanket of white, he thought to himself. The only time it looked prettier was when it was sprouting the greens and reds and yellows and oranges of brightly colored vegetables.

Gopher's head emerged cautiously from the mouth of one of his numerous burrows and was instantly covered with a fine dusting of white snow, like sugar on a doughnut. He whistled, impressed by the amount of snow that was now tumbling from the sky. He smiled. A layer of snow on the ground always made his winter's sleep all the cozier. Gopher yawned in relaxed anticipation of the long nap to come.

Piglet was fiercely sweeping his walk, but the white curtain of

winter was now descending much too quickly. As soon as he'd cleared one section of his front walk, another was buried in snow. With an exasperated sigh, Piglet leaned wearily on his broom and watched the snow gather in sparkling piles of white all over his walkway.

"Well," the very small animal told himself with a smile, "at least it's very clean snow. It would be a pity if I had to wash it and pile it up myself." He giggled into his hand at such an idea and continued to observe the soft accumulation of white powder.

And Tigger was no sooner aware of the cascading snowflakes than he was out making snow tiggers in the ice-cold fluff.

"'Cuz that's what tiggers do best when it's snowifying," he said, then added a "Hoo-hoo-*hoo*!" for good measure.

Meanwhile, Eeyore watched the swirling, twirling, and wildly somersaulting snowflakes with a rueful smile.

"Well," he said, rumbling to himself, "at least the holes in my roof will have something to let inside the house. That'll make 'em happy."

And then the donkey smiled, because there was no one around to see it and because he was so fond of snow that he truly didn't mind its sharing his house with him.

Then, quite suddenly, on every face all over the Hundred-Acre Wood—from Pooh Bear to Piglet to Eeyore—a realization popped open their eyes and mouths in amazement as they all thought the same thought at once!

"Oh my goodness," said Pooh.

"It's snowing . . ." began Rabbit.

"...and that means..." the flabbergasted Gopher said to himself.

"...that it's almost Christmas," finished the suddenly very nervous Piglet.

"And Christmas means..." said Tigger with a gasp, rubbing his head in wonder.

"...that there are presents to be delivered," said Eeyore, "and not much time to deliver 'em in!"

It wasn't very long at all before everyone was crisscrossing through the Hundred-Acre Wood, loaded down with presents that they left at one another's homes. By the time everything had been delivered, however, the snowstorm had turned into a blizzard, a

whirling waterfall of white, falling so thickly and blowing so fiercely that it was impossible to tell whether there was a path underfoot or a tree in front of a nose. As a result, there were quite a number of misplaced paths, bumped trees, and bruised noses by the time all the presents had been properly placed.

In fact, the only one who wasn't having any trouble finding his way home in the blowing snow and falling darkness was little Roo. But then that wasn't so very unusual. Home was where his Mama waited for him, and nothing as minor as a howling blizzard can keep a child away from his mother.

But as he hopped along, each bounce jarring off the snow that tried to cling to him, Roo came across a strange sight. There was a snowman standing in the middle of what used to be the path before it was covered with snow, pondering in a very Pooh Bear sort of way.

"Hello," said Roo in surprise, shouting to be heard over the roar of the storm.

"Why, hello, Roo," the snowman shouted back, which surprised Roo even more because he could not recall ever hearing a snowman talk before, let alone call him by name. And he spoke in a voice that sounded very much like Pooh's!

"But that must be the storm playing tricks," said Roo. "Why else would a snowman sound like Winnie the Pooh?"

"I seem," shouted the snowman, "to be having a bit of a

bother finding my way home in this storm!"

"Why don't you come home with me?" suggested Roo at the top of his voice.

"What a good idea," responded the snowman agreeably. "I suppose any home is a good home in the middle of a storm."

So Roo continued to hop toward home, with the snowman stomping along behind on his short stubby legs.

But the evening's surprises were not over for Roo. Another snowman appeared out of the gloom, with long attachments on his head like feelers on a caterpillar. At Roo's invitation to join them, the second snowman, who was shivering so badly that he couldn't speak, nodded in happy acceptance. Roo found this very strange. "Who ever heard of a snowman who got too cold?" he asked himself.

"It must have something to do with Christmas Eve," Roo concluded. He was certain the magic of the holiday had to have something to do with these walking, talking, too cold snow creatures.

The next snow being they came across had four legs and two heads! The second head appeared to be a very small animal with large ears sitting atop the first droopy-eared creature. Wow! thought the amazed Roo. Whoever made that snowman certainly had a lot of imagination!

The last snowperson who joined the procession to Roo's house carried another little snow creature in his arms that whistled when he talked. The voice sounded familiar, but Roo was getting tired and wanted to get home, so he didn't try very hard to figure out who he was reminded of.

And the snowman holding the whistler had a long tail. Roo noticed that the snowman kept trying to hop. Roo was pleased to think that snowmen hopped, too, but this one wasn't very successful at hopping because of the snowman he was carrying in his arms.

When, at last, Roo saw the lights of his house shining brightly through the snow, he dashed ahead and flung open the door.

"Mama!" he shouted. "I'm home just like I promised!"

Kanga ran out to meet him. "Good for you, dear," she said, smiling. Then she began brushing snow from her son. "You look almost like a snowman," she said, laughing.

"I brought home some company!" Roo exclaimed, excitedly pointing to the snow creatures on the porch. "See?"

"How nice," responded Kanga. Much to her son's surprise,

she was not at all surprised by the sight of Roo's guests.

"I'll take care of our visitors," Kanga told Roo as she pushed him toward his bedroom, "while you get out of those wet clothes and put on some warm pajamas."

Roo was very anxious to ask the snow creatures about Christmas and magic and the best snow for snow-balls, so he changed in no time at all.

But when he ran back into the parlor, the snowmen were gone! Sitting next to the fire, with pools of water puddling at their feet, were his friends Pooh, Rabbit, Piglet, Eeyore, Gopher, and Tigger, sipping mugs of hot chocolate in front of a cozy fire, looking very contented indeed.

"Where . . . ?" Roo sputtered, looking around in disappointment. "Where are all the snowmen?"

"What snowmen, Roo, dear?" asked Kanga, with a quizzical look on her face.

"The ones who followed me home!" he wailed. "The magic ones that could walk and talk and shiver because it was Christmas Eve!"

"Oh," responded Rabbit, exchanging knowing looks with the others. "*Those* snowmen."

"Er . . . it was much too warm for them in here," blurted out Piglet nervously.

"Yeah," Tigger agreed. "They had to go back outside in the cold coolness."

"After all," Gopher said with a whistle, "they have a lot to do and only one night a year to do it in."

"They were sorry they couldn't say good-bye," rumbled Eeyore.

"Oh bother," said Pooh, sighing sadly, "I'm sorry I missed them, too."

"Oh well," said Roo in a very disappointed voice. "At least I got to meet them."

"And there's always next year, Roo," said Pooh sympathetically, putting his arm around Roo's shoulders. "Perhaps I'll get to meet them then, too."

Kanga patted her son's head. "I'm certain they were glad to have met you, Roo dear," she said.

"No doubt about *that*," sniffed Rabbit. "And just in the nick of time!"

"And they won't forget ya, kid," announced Tigger.

"They won't?" said Roo, brightening. "Are you sure?"

"As sure as my name is T-I-double-Guh-Rrr!"

So, that night, after the snow had ceased falling and he'd said good night to everyone, Roo went to bed. He was very happy and dreamed good dreams about his new friends and hoped they had a wonderful Christmas Eve doing whatever it was snowmen did on Christmas Eve. But, most of all, he hoped he'd meet them again sometime.

And when Roo awoke Christmas morning, he not only discovered presents under his tree but also found a yard full of snowmen outside the front door. Around them were the familiar footprints of

his friends—circling, crossing, and intersecting. Roo knew that there was no better place to spend Christmas than at his house. (And the snowmen, after a magical Christmas Eve, obviously knew it, too.)

Even if he never saw the walking and talking and shivering snowmen again, he'd never forget them.

And, after all, aren't good memories and magic what Christmas is all about?

Sledding with Christopher Robin

Down the slippery, slidey slope
Go Christopher Robin and I.

Over a hump, bumpity bump,
Watch out for that tree—oh my!

Into a curving, swerving turn,
We lean out far to the right.

Back to a tipping, whipping pace,
We sail on an ocean of white.

Then there's a slowing, swishing sound
As we finally glide to a stop.

For one more slippery, slidey ride
We hike back up to the top.

The Best Part of Christmas

What's the best part of Christmas?

The gifts?

The cookies?

The tree?

No, the best part of Christmas
Is that you share it with me!

Pooh's Wishing Star

The newly fallen snow squeaked under the shifting feet of Christopher Robin and Winnie the Pooh, as they climbed to the top of their hill. The Bear of Very Little Brain looked in awe at the star whose cheerful sparkling lit and colored the cold night sky.

"Christopher Robin," said the very impressed bear, "is that twinkly one really your very own wishing star? REALLY?"

"Absolutely!" Christopher Robin said, laughing. "Would you like to wish for something?"

"Oh my, yes!" responded Pooh.

"First, you're going to have to say the very special wishing rhyme," explained Christopher Robin, and he recited,

> Flap like a bird,
> Jump like a fish,
> Stand up, sit down,
> Wish-wish-WISH!

"Now cover your eyes, Pooh Bear, and make your wish!"

Closing his eyes and smacking his lips, Pooh said, "I wish I had something sweet . . . for ME!"

Christopher Robin quickly brought a pot of honey out from hiding and placed it at Pooh's feet.

At the sight of the honeypot, Pooh launched into a mouthful of wishes. "My goodness! I wish for a pot of honey for Piglet . . . and one for me. A pot for Rabbit . . . and another one for me . . . and . . ."

"You don't want to do that, Pooh," interrupted Christopher Robin quickly. "It's a very small wishing star," he explained, "and too many wishes might wear it out."

"Oh," said Pooh, drooping. Then a thought came to him (as thoughts usually did when the possibility of more honey was concerned), and he added, "Can we come back tomorrow night?"

"Of course we can," Christopher Robin said with a laugh.

Pooh waved a polite good-bye to the twinkling star and chuckled. "I think he winked at me," he said.

The next morning found Pooh slurping his wished-for pot of honey. But all at once, the slurping stopped.

"Is there anything sadder than an empty pot of honey?" Pooh Bear asked himself.

Then it all came back to him!

"I'll simply have to wish another wish, and . . ." His brow furrowed as an unhappy thought tickled the back of his head full of fluff.

"Oh dear," he groaned. "I think I remember that I've forgotten the wishing rhyme! This," he told himself, "is going to take some very large think-think-THINKING!"

Later, Pooh was strolling through the woods, hoping that his think-think-thinker would work better if he wasn't sitting down on it.

"Hop like a banana, jump like a bean . . ." he mumbled to himself. "No," he said, sighing, "that isn't it."

At that very moment, Pooh's very small friend Piglet was pushing a snowball up a hill. As the snowball grew larger and larger, Piglet pushed more and more slowly. Until finally, picking up the very small animal, the huge snowball rolled him back down the hill!

"Oh d-dear!" Piglet cried as Pooh was swept up in the rolling snowball, too!

The snowball burst open with a loud thump when it hit a tree and left the surprised Pooh and Piglet looking at each other in snow-covered wonder.

Pooh was explaining his predicament to Piglet when they happened upon Tigger playing checkers with himself.

"Hoo-hoo-*hoo!*" he hooted as he trounced himself yet again. "I win, I win! Oh I always win. If only there were two o' me, then things'd be FUN!"

"Why, hello, Tigger!" Pooh said.

"Pooh Bear!" shouted Tigger. "Wanna play?"

"We can't, Tigger," explained Piglet. "We're going to wish on Christopher Robin's wishing star!"

"A wishing star!" exclaimed Tigger. "Can I pretty please with anchovies on it go and wish for another tigger?"

"Well, you see," began Pooh, "I can't—"

Tigger threw his arms around the startled bear. "Thanks, buddy bear!"

So the three of them went on together, traipsing through the
woods as Pooh tried to remember what he'd forgotten. "Flap like
an armadillo, hoot like a goose . . . Oh BOTHER bother."

No one was more surprised than the three friends
when they came upon Rabbit fending off an army
of bugs with a frying pan.

"Oh no!" shouted Tigger. "Rabbit's outnumbered
a jillion to one! What'll we do?"

"Build a snowman?" suggested Piglet.

It wasn't long before Piglet's attempt at another giant
snowball had chased the bugs away and left the four friends
covered with snow and sitting next to a tree.

Rabbit was very grateful that the bugs had been sent packing.
"But," he moaned, "I wish there were some way to keep them
away for good!"

Piglet and Tigger wasted no time in informing Rabbit
of Pooh's wishing star.

"How wonderful," said Rabbit.

"If only I could remember the wishing rhyme," said Pooh.

"Don't fret, Pooh Bear," said Tigger. "We'll cure you."

First, Rabbit tried "scaring" Pooh's memory back. "It works for hiccups, doesn't it?" he asked with a sniff.

Not to be defeated, Tigger quickly stood Pooh on his head.

"Memories all flow down to his footsies," he explained. "Do you remember who I am, buddy bear?"

"Why, yes," said Pooh. "You're Tigger."

"It worked! It worked!" declared Tigger.

"But," Pooh interrupted Tigger, "I always remember who you are, Tigger."

"Oh yeah, I forgot," said the embarrassed Tigger.

Tigger and Rabbit decided to tie a hot water bottle to Pooh's head in order to warm the memories up, but began to argue about whether Pooh should sit down or stand up while he was waiting for things to get warm.

"Sit down!" announced Tigger.

"Stand up," countered Rabbit.

And suddenly, it all came back to Pooh Bear!

"Flap like a bird, jump like a fish, stand up, sit down, wish-wish-WISH!" he recited happily.

"C'mon, gang! Let's go wishifryin'!" shouted Tigger.

"I really want to make that wish," Pooh told himself as
he hurried after the others. "I do hope I'm not too late."

Winnie the Pooh arrived on top of the knoll to find his friends all wishing their wishes!

"I wish there was another tigger," said Tigger.

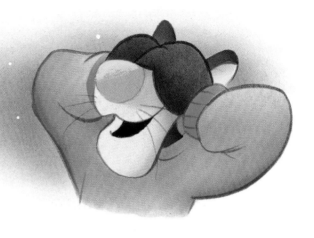

"I wish those bugs would go away for ever and ever!" pleaded Rabbit.

"I w-wish I could build a snowman all by myself," said Piglet very politely.

As they left, everyone thanked Pooh for sharing the wishing star.

"I wonder," Pooh asked himself, "how many wishes a wishing star can give?"

As Pooh Bear closed his eyes and concentrated on repeating the wishing rhyme, he didn't notice the sky filling with clouds.

"I wish," he said finally, "for a small—but not TOO small—smackerel of something sweet."

But when Pooh opened his eyes, the star was gone. Suddenly, out of the corner of his eye, he saw a star shoot to the ground in a blazing streak!

"Oh no!" cried the distressed bear. "Christopher Robin's star! I wished it OUT!"

As Pooh walked down the knoll, he didn't see the clouds disperse behind him and the wishing star twinkling as brightly as ever.

"I used it up before my friends' wishes could come true, too," Pooh glumly reminded himself.

"There's only one thing to do!" he announced. "If the wishing star can't make their wishes come true, then I WILL! I hope."

The next day Pooh pretended very hard to be Piglet's snowman,

another tigger for Tigger,

and a bug wrangler for Rabbit
all at the same time.

But the effort was all too much for one not very fast-moving
bear.

"This wish-come-true-ing is very tiring," said the weary
Pooh Bear. "No wonder the wishing star got pooped."

It wasn't long before his friends realized what was going on.
With a little coaxing, they finally got the whole story from a very
sorry Pooh Bear.

"But, Pooh," the suddenly anxious Piglet asked, "what will happen when Christopher Robin comes to make a wish?"

After an anxious moment of his own, Pooh became very serious. "There's going to be a wishing star out tonight, or my name's not Winnie the Pooh!"

Before the night grew very much older, Pooh was dressed up as the wishing star—each limb a point and one more for the top of his head full of fluff. Then he was carefully perched on a bent-over sapling.

"Do you think," Pooh asked the others, "that if I'm far enough away, Christopher Robin will believe I'm the wishing star?"

"Just remember to look twinkly," suggested Tigger.

"Are you very sure about this, Pooh Bear?" asked Rabbit.

"Well . . ." began Pooh thoughtfully.

But before he could finish, Tigger released the sapling, sending Pooh flying into the night sky.

Pooh didn't fly as very far up as he thought he would. In fact, he ended up dangling from a tree limb, and there was Christopher Robin walking up the knoll below him.

"Uh, hello, Christopher Robin," said Pooh. "Er, the wishing star—that's me—is over here tonight."

"So you are," Christopher Robin agreed. "But why?"

"Why?" babbled Pooh. "Er, I came down for a closer look, and this tree grabbed me and—um—oh, do make a wish."

"All right," said Christopher Robin. "Flap like a bird, jump like a fish, stand up, sit down, wish-wish-WISH!

"I wish my best friend were beside me," he announced.

At that precise moment, Pooh's costume decided that it had hung up in that tree long enough. The next thing Pooh knew, he had fallen into Christopher Robin's arms!

"Why, Pooh Bear!" exclaimed Christopher Robin. "My wish came true."

"How can that be?" said a not-a-little-confused Pooh. "I didn't listen to you, and I wore out your wishing star."

"Silly old bear," said Christopher Robin with a laugh. "Look."

Pooh looked up into a sky empty of clouds where the wishing star was the brightest star of all.

"You mean it was there all the time?" asked Pooh.

"Didn't your friends' wishes all come true?" asked Christopher Robin.

"Yes," answered Pooh, "sort of. But I thought I did them."

"Perhaps with a little help from the wishing star," suggested Christopher Robin.

"Stars certainly are smart," said Pooh.

"Let's go home, Pooh Bear," said Christopher Robin.

"Just one moment," said Pooh. "I want to thank the wishing star."

"Me, too, Pooh," Christopher Robin said, smiling.

And on the snow-covered knoll beneath the twinkling star, the boy and the bear silently thanked the wishing star for their most important wish come true—each other!

Jingle Bells

Dashing through the snow,
In a one-horse open sleigh,

O'er the fields we go,
Laughing all the way!

Bells on bobtail ring,
Making spirits bright,

What fun it is
to ride and sing
A sleighing song
tonight!

Jingle bells! Jingle bells!
Jingle all the way!
Oh, what fun
it is to ride
In a one-horse
open sleigh!

Christmas Eve Lullaby

It's Christmas Eve, my baby.
It's Christmas Eve, my Roo.
Outside the snow is falling
And making the world look new.

Come sit on my lap, my baby.
Come lean your head back, my Roo.
Just close your eyes and listen
While I sing you a carol or two.

Shhh, sleep safely, my baby.
Shhh, sleep soundly, my Roo.
Christmas morning is coming.
Soon all your dreams will come true.

Merry Christmas, Winnie the Pooh!

One snowy Christmas Eve, Winnie the Pooh looked up and down, in and out, and all around his house.

"I have a tree, some candles, and lots of decorations,"
he said, "but *something* seems to be missing."

Rap-a-tap-tap! A sudden small knocking made Pooh think that whatever was missing might be just outside his door.

But when Pooh opened the door, a small snowman stood shaking on his step.

"H-Hello, P-Pooh," said the snowman in a shivery, quivery, but oh-so-familiar voice. "The only thing I don't like about Christmas is that my ears get so very cold."

After much melting
by Pooh's cozy fireplace,
the snowman looked less
like a snowman and
more like Piglet!

"My!" said Pooh,
happy to see a friend
where there used to be a
snowman.

"My!" said Piglet, now
warm enough to see
Pooh's glowing Christmas
tree.

"Are you going to string popcorn for your tree?" asked Piglet.

"There *was* popcorn and string," admitted Pooh. "But now there's only string."

"Then we can use the string to wrap the presents you're giving," Piglet said with a laugh.

Something began to tickle at the brain of the little bear. "I forgot to get presents!" exclaimed Pooh.

"Don't worry, Pooh," said Piglet, trying to smile bravely. "It's the thought that counts." Soon Piglet left to wrap his own presents.

Pooh didn't know what to do about the forgotten presents, but he did know where to find help.

"Hello!" called Pooh, knocking on Christopher Robin's door.

"Come in, Pooh," said Christopher Robin, smiling. "Why do you look sad on the most wonderful night of the year?"

But Pooh had forgotten all about the presents, again. "What are those?" he asked, pointing to some stockings hung by the fireplace.

"Those are stockings to hold Christmas presents," explained Christopher Robin. Poor Pooh suddenly remembered that he didn't have presents — or stockings.

Luckily, the bear of little brain was smart enough to have a good friend. Christopher Robin gave Pooh stockings for himself and all of his friends.

Pooh thanked Christopher Robin and hurried off to deliver the stockings. "I will get everyone presents later," Pooh said to himself. "The stockings come first."

With a small note that said
"From Pooh," he left a stocking for

Piglet,

Tigger,

Rabbit,

Eeyore,

Gopher,

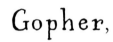

and Owl.

Back at his own comfy house, Pooh said, "Now I must think about presents for my friends." But sleepy Pooh's thinking soon turned into dreaming.

Thump-a-bump-bump!
The next morning, Pooh
was awakened by a big and
bouncy knock at his door.
"Merry Christmas, Pooh!"
shouted his friends.

Pooh opened the door. He was about to apologize for not having any presents to give when Piglet, Tigger, Rabbit, Gopher, Eeyore, and Owl started *thanking* him.

"No more cold ears with my new stocking cap," said Piglet.

"My stripedy sleeping bag is tigger-ific!" exclaimed Tigger.

"So is my new carrot cover," Rabbit chimed in.

Gopher thanked Pooh for the rock-collecting bag. Eeyore happily swished his toasty tail-warmer.

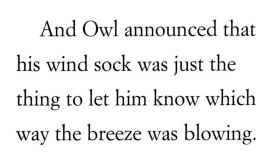

And Owl announced that his wind sock was just the thing to let him know which way the breeze was blowing.

"Something awfully nice is going on," said Pooh. "But I'm not sure how it happened."

"It's called Christmas, buddy bear," replied Tigger. Then everyone gave presents to Pooh: lots of pots of honey.

Surrounded by his friends and his favorite tasty treats, Pooh had to agree. "Christmas! What a sweet thought, indeed."